The Howling Himalayan and Pepe at Worthwyle

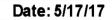

Written by
Angela DeFina

Dedicated to my Loving Family:

Joseph, my great Father, was
always there even to solve any
problems that might arise.
Josephine, my great Mother, who
was always there for me also
in any hardship of my life.
Joseph, my great Brother, who
always makes me laugh when I
need it and is a great help.
Pamela, my great Sister, is
beautiful inside and out and saved
my life when I needed it.

Every morning before Pepe,
the mother, will rise
the Himalayan howls and looks Pepe
straight in the eyes.

The howls can be heard throughout
the house called Worthwyle
and Pepe says "ssssshhh" because
that is the mama's style.

The Himalayan retreats and goes
back to sleep
and Pepe smiles victorious without
saying a peep.

Once again the Himalayan howls
and Pepe rises out of the bed
without any scowls.

Brother Andy in the next room
hopes the howling will stop soon
Sister Pam in her room
asks from her bed
that the Himalayan stop howling
and be happy instead.

Pepe puts on her robe and slippers
and steps down the stair
for to keep the Himalayan howling
would not be fair.

For what the Himalayan wants is
her plate of food on the floor
and Pepe places the plate of food
on the floor
smiling all the while,
because it is no chore.

Down the street the
Himalayan scampered
away from the house where
she did get pampered.

Pepe and Good neighbor Sam
see the Himalayan is lost
they must find the kitty
at whatever cost.

Good neighbor Sam finds
the Himalayan
he returns it to Worthwyle where
the family is praying.

Good neighbor Sam, Pepe,
Brother Andy, and
Sister Pam agree
that what makes everything
so wonderful
at Worthwyle to see

Is thoughtfulness and love
virtues to practice all of life
for you and me.